ISBN 1 85854 090 9
© Brimax Books Ltd 1994. All rights reserved.
Published by Brimax Books Ltd, Newmarket, England, 1994.
Reprinted 1994
Printed in China

Fairy Tales

ILLUSTRATED BY ERIC KINCAID

BRIMAX • NEWMARKET • ENGLAND

Contents

Hansel and Gretel

Once there was a woodcutter. He was very poor. One day he said to his wife, "What will become of us? We are so poor we cannot feed the children."

His wife said, "We will take the children into the forest and leave them there. They must take care of themselves."

Hansel and Gretel were listening at the door. Gretel began to cry. "What will become of us?" she said.

"Do not cry," said Hansel. "I will look after you."

When it was dark Hansel went into the garden. He filled his pockets with pebbles. Then he went to bed.

Next day the woodcutter took the children into the forest. His wife gave them both a piece of bread. Hansel's pockets were full of pebbles. Gretel had to put the bread in her apron.

Hansel kept looking back at the house. "What are you looking at?" asked the woodcutter.

"I am looking at my little cat," said Hansel. But really he was dropping pebbles on the path.

When they were deep in the forest the woodcutter made a fire. "Sit and rest," he said to Hansel and Gretel. "When we have cut the wood we will come back for you."

Hansel and Gretel waited and waited. Their father did not return. At last they went to sleep.

When Hansel and Gretel woke, it was dark. They were alone. Gretel began to cry.

"Do not cry," said Hansel. "As soon as the moon rises, I will take you home."

The moonlight shone on the pebbles Hansel had dropped on the path. They followed them all the way home.

Some days later Hansel and Gretel heard their stepmother plotting again. When she was asleep, Hansel went to fill his pockets with pebbles. The door was locked. He could not get into the garden. Gretel began to cry.

"Do not cry," said Hansel. "I will think of something."

Next morning their stepmother gave them both a piece of bread. Hansel put his bread into his pocket. He broke it into crumbs.

"Why do you always look back?" asked the woodcutter.

"I am watching my pigeon," said Hansel. But really he was dropping crumbs along the path.

The children were left as before. The moon rose. Hansel looked for the crumbs. They were not there. Birds had eaten them. Now Hansel and Gretel were lost.

Three days passed. Then they saw a white bird. "It wants us to follow it," said Hansel.

Hansel and Gretel followed the bird. It led them to a house with walls made of gingerbread. It had a roof made of cake and windows made of sugar.

Hansel and Gretel were hungry. They broke off a piece of the house. They began to eat.

"Nibble nibble like a mouse. Who is nibbling at my house?" said a voice. The children thought it was the wind and took no notice.

The door of the house opened. An old woman came out. The old woman asked them into the house. She gave them food to eat and a bed to sleep in.

The children thought she was kind. She was really a witch. She had made the gingerbread house to trap children. She ate children for dinner.

The witch shut Hansel in a stable. It had bars in the door. Then the witch woke Gretel. "Cook something for your brother," she said. "I want to fatten him up before I eat him."

Gretel wept, but she had to do as she was told.

Hansel was given the best food. Gretel was given the scraps. Every day the witch made Hansel put his finger through the bars. Every day Hansel held out a bone instead of his finger. The witch could not see very well. Every day she said, "Not fat enough yet!"

One day the witch could wait no longer. "Fetch some water, girl. Fill the pot!" she said. When that was done, she said, "Crawl into the oven, girl. Make sure it is hot." The witch was going to push Gretel into the oven.

Gretel guessed what the witch was going to do. "I do not know how to get into the oven," she said.

"Silly girl!" said the witch. "I will show you."

Gretel stood behind the witch. She pushed the witch into the oven. She closed the door. It only took a moment to free Hansel. They filled their pockets with treasure from the witch's house. Then they set off to find their way home. A white duck took them part of the way.

At last they came to a part of the forest they knew. Soon they saw their own house.

The woodcutter was very glad to see them. He told them their stepmother was dead.

They sold the treasure and the three of them lived happily ever after.

Town Mouse and Country Mouse

Once there were two mice. One mouse lived in a house in the middle of a town. He was called the town mouse.

The second mouse lived in the country. His house was on the edge of a field. He was called the country mouse.

The town mouse and the country mouse met one day at a wedding. They soon became friends.

One day the country mouse sent a letter to the town mouse. It said, "Would you like to come and stay with me in the country?"

The town mouse was pleased. He had never been to the country. He packed his bag. He went to the country the same day.

The country mouse was waiting for him. "Please come in," said the country mouse.

The country mouse showed the town mouse his house. It did not take long. His house was very small. The country mouse liked his small house. It was cosy. The town mouse thought it a bit TOO small.

The country mouse got some food ready. There was barleycorn and roots. The country mouse had roots every day. Roots and barleycorn were the only food he had. He was used to them. He liked them. The town mouse did not like them at all. He pulled a face.

The town mouse felt sorry for the country mouse. He would not like to live in a small house. He would not like to eat roots all the time. "Come to the town and stay with me," said the town mouse. "I will show you what good living is about."

The country mouse packed his bag. He locked the door of his house. Then he went to the town with the town mouse.

The country mouse had never been to the town. It was very busy. They came to some steps. "What a big house," said the country mouse.

"This is where I live," said the town mouse. "Come in."

The town mouse took the country mouse to the larder. The country mouse gasped. He had never seen so much food in one place. There was flour and oatmeal, figs and honey and dates.

"Help yourself," said the town mouse.

"Can I?" said the country mouse.

"Of course you can," said the town mouse. "Eat whatever you like."

The country mouse liked the look of the dates. He had never seen a date before. He sniffed it. It smelt good.

The country mouse nibbled at the date. He liked the taste.

Suddenly the town mouse pricked up his ears. "Quick!" said the town mouse. "Someone is coming. We must hide." The two mice ran and hid in a tiny hole.

They waited until it was safe to come out. They seemed to wait a long time. The country mouse did not like hiding. He wanted to eat that date. At last the town mouse said it was safe to leave the hole.

The country mouse finished the date. He started to eat a fig.

Suddenly the town mouse pricked up his ears. "Quick!" said the town mouse. "We must hide. Someone is coming!"

The two mice hid again. "Does this happen often?" asked the country mouse.

"Oh, all the time," said the town mouse. "You will soon get used to it."

"I do not want to get used to it," said the country mouse. "I do not like running to hide when I am eating. It makes my tummy ache. I am going home."

The country mouse was very glad to be home. He might have only roots to eat, but at least he could eat them in peace.

Thumbelina

Once there was a woman who wanted a child. She went to see a witch. The witch gave her a barleycorn. It was a very special barleycorn.

The woman took the barleycorn home and planted it. It grew into a flower like a tulip. The petals were tightly closed.

The woman kissed the petals. They opened. Inside the flower was a tiny girl no bigger than the woman's thumb. The woman called the child Thumbelina.

Thumbelina slept in a cradle made from a walnut shell. The covers were made from flower petals. Thumbelina played in a boat made from a tulip petal.

One day an ugly toad hopped through the window. The toad wanted Thumbelina as a wife for her son. The toad carried the cradle away. Thumbelina was asleep inside it.

The toad put the cradle on a lily leaf. She went to get a room ready under the mud.

When Thumbelina awoke she was afraid. Soon the toad came back. She took the cradle to the room. She left Thumbelina sitting on the lily leaf.

The fish did not like to see Thumbelina cry. They nibbled through the lily stem. The leaf floated down the river. Thumbelina went with it.

A butterfly pulled the leaf some of the way. A big beetle picked Thumbelina up. It took her to a tree.

The other beetles thought Thumbelina was ugly. "Let her go," they said. The beetle put Thumbelina down on a daisy.

Thumbelina stayed in the wood. She lived by herself. But she was never lonely. The birds were her friends. Her clothes were tattered and torn, but she was never cold. She was happy all day long.

Then winter came. The wind was very cold. Thumbelina tried to keep warm. Snow began to fall. Thumbelina wrapped herself in a leaf. If she did not find somewhere warm to stay she would die.

Thumbelina went into a field where the corn had been cut. She knocked at a door. A field mouse opened it and asked her in. "You can stay with me as long as you like," said the field mouse.

The mole came on a visit. He said he would like to marry Thumbelina. Thumbelina and the field mouse went to see the mole's house. The mole led them along a dark tunnel. On the way they passed a swallow. It was lying very still. "It's dead!" said the mole. He pushed the swallow with his foot.

Thumbelina could not forget the swallow. She waited until the others were asleep. Then she went back to the tunnel.

She lay her head on the swallow's chest. Its heart was beating. It was not dead. It had fainted because it was so cold. Thumbelina covered it up to make it as warm as she could.

Thumbelina went back to the swallow the next night. It had opened its eyes. Thumbelina looked after the swallow all winter long. It grew well and strong.

Spring came. Thumbelina made a hole in the roof of the tunnel. Now the swallow could fly away.

"Sit on my back and I will take you with me," said the swallow.

"I cannot," said Thumbelina. "I am to marry the mole." She watched sadly as the swallow flew away.

The wedding day drew near. Thumbelina sat all day at the spinning wheel, spinning thread for her wedding dress. Thumbelina was unhappy. She did not like the mole. She did not want to marry him. She did not want to live underground for the rest of her life.

It was Thumbelina's wedding day. The mole said she could take one last look at the sun. Thumbelina looked up at the sky for the last time. She heard someone call.

It was the swallow. "Come, fly with me!" said the swallow. This time Thumbelina did.

The swallow took Thumbelina to the place where the swallows make their nests. Near the nests were some white flowers. Living inside the flowers were tiny people like herself.

Thumbelina married the King of the tiny people. She wore a golden crown. She was given a pair of wings as a wedding present. Thumbelina changed her name to Maia and lived happily ever after.

The Wizard of Oz

Dorothy lived with her Aunt Em and Uncle Henry. She had a small dog called Toto.

One day there was a whirlwind. Dorothy and Toto were alone in the house. The whirlwind lifted them up high into the sky. The house came to rest in the Land of the Munchkins. It fell on top of the Wicked Witch of the East and killed her.

The Munchkins were very pleased. They gave Dorothy the Wicked Witch of the East's magic shoes.

"Can you help me find my way home?" she asked the Munchkins. They shook their heads. They did not know the way.

"Go to the Emerald City," they said. "Ask the Wizard of Oz to help you."

Dorothy put on the magic shoes and set off along the yellow brick road with Toto.

After many miles Dorothy met a Scarecrow. "Can I go to the Emerald City with you?" said the Scarecrow. "Perhaps the Wizard of Oz will give me a brain."

The next day they found a Tin Man in the forest. "Can I go with you?" said the Tin Man. "Perhaps the Wizard of Oz will give me a heart."

A Lion jumped out of the bushes and roared. It tried to bite Toto. Dorothy slapped the Lion. "How dare you bite a

26

little dog! You are a coward!" said Dorothy.

"I know," said the Lion. "But how can I help it? Do you think the Wizard of Oz would give me some courage?"

They went across ditches and over rivers. At last they came to the Land of Oz. They went to the Emerald City. Everything in the city was green.

The Wizard of Oz lived in a palace. He was a magician. He could change the way he looked.

In the Throne Room all Dorothy could see was a huge green head. "I am Oz," said a voice. "Who are you and why do you seek me?"

Dorothy told him she wanted to find the way home.

"I will help if you kill the Wicked Witch of the West," said the Wizard.

The Scarecrow saw the Wizard as a green lady. The Tin Man saw the Wizard as a wild animal. The Lion saw him as a ball of fire.

They all got the same answer from the Wizard. He would help if they killed the Wicked Witch of the West.

The Wicked Witch of the West saw them coming. She tried to stop them.

The Tin Man killed the wolves. The Scarecrow caught the crows. The bees broke their stings when they tried to sting the Tin Man. The Winkies ran away when the Lion roared.

The Wicked Witch of the West was angry. She sent the fierce Flying Monkeys after them. They dropped the Tin Man on to some rocks. He broke into pieces. They pulled the straw out of the Scarecrow. They put the Lion into a cage.

The Flying Monkeys took Dorothy and Toto to the Wicked Witch's castle. The Witch saw Dorothy's magic shoes and began to shake. The Wicked Witch kicked Toto. That made Dorothy very angry.

She picked up a bucket of water and threw it over the Witch. Then as Dorothy looked on in wonder, the Witch began to shrink and fall away. Then there was nothing but a puddle. The Wicked Witch of the West was dead.

Dorothy let the Lion out of the cage. The Winkies helped her put the straw back into the Scarecrow. They helped her put the Tin Man back together.

When they returned to the palace the Throne Room was empty. The Lion gave a roar and knocked over a screen. Hiding behind it was a little man. It was the Wizard. "I am not really a wizard," he said. "People only think I am because I can do tricks. But I will help you if I can."

The Wizard filled the Scarecrow's head with sharp things like pins and needles. "Now you have a brain," he said.

He took a red silk heart stuffed with sawdust and put it inside the Tin Man.

He gave the Lion a drink that would give him courage.

He made a balloon so that Dorothy and Toto could fly home. The balloon took off before Dorothy was ready. It flew away without her.

The Good Witch of the South came to rescue Dorothy. "Tap your heels together three times and tell the magic shoes where you want to go," she said.

The Good Witch of the South made the Scarecrow ruler of the Emerald City. She made the Tin Man ruler of the Winkies. She made the Lion King of the Forest.

Dorothy and Toto went home to Aunt Em and Uncle Henry.

Cinderella

Cinderella lived in a big house. She was always busy. Her two stepsisters made her work hard.

"Cinderella! Sweep the floor!"

"Cinderella! Wash the dishes!"

"Make the beds!"

"Clean the windows!"

Cinderella's work was never done. Her stepsisters spent half the day telling Cinderella what to do. They spent the other half trying to make themselves pretty.

"Cinderella! Brush my hair!"

"Cinderella! Tie my bow!"

"Powder my nose!"

"Fasten my buttons!"

One day a letter arrived at the house. "There is to be a ball at the palace. We are invited!" shouted the stepsisters.

"Am I invited?" asked Cinderella.

"Even if you are, you cannot go," said her stepsisters. "You will be too busy getting us ready."

The day of the ball came. The stepsisters kept Cinderella very busy indeed. There was so much to do. Poor Cinderella did not know what to do first.

At last, the stepsisters had gone and the house was quiet. Cinderella sat by the fire and began to cry. "If only I

could go to the ball," she wept.

"You SHALL go to the ball," said a voice behind her.

Cinderella jumped up in surprise. She thought she was alone in the house.

"Who ... who are you?" she gasped.

"I am your Fairy Godmother," said the stranger. "I have come to get you ready for the ball."

"Bring me a pumpkin," said the Fairy Godmother. She turned the pumpkin into a coach.

"Bring me four white mice," said the Fairy Godmother. She turned the mice into four white horses.

"Bring me three lizards," said the Fairy Godmother. They became a coach-driver and two footmen.

"I cannot go to the ball dressed in rags," said Cinderella sadly.

The Fairy Godmother waved her magic wand once more. Cinderella's rags turned into a beautiful ballgown. Her bare feet were covered with dainty glass slippers.

"Now you are ready for the ball," said the Fairy God-mother. "But first, a warning. You must leave before the clock strikes twelve. At twelve everything will change back again."

"I will remember," said Cinderella. "Thank you, dear Fairy Godmother."

Cinderella danced all night with the Prince. Her step-sisters saw her, but they did not know it was Cinderella. They thought she was a princess.

Cinderella was so happy she forgot all about the Fairy Godmother's warning. Then the palace clock began to strike the chimes of midnight. One ... two ... three ...

"I must go!" cried Cinderella and she ran from the palace.

"Stop! Stop!" cried the Prince.

Cinderella did not hear him. As she ran down the palace steps she lost one of her glass slippers. ... ten ... eleven ... TWELVE!!!

The beautiful gown turned into rags. The coach turned into a pumpkin. The mice and the lizards ran away.

The Prince found her glass slipper lying on the palace steps. He called to a footman. "Take this slipper and find its owner. I will marry the girl it fits."

The footman travelled all over the kingdom with the slipper. It fitted no one. At last he came to the house where Cinderella lived.

"Let me try it!" said one of the stepsisters. She snatched the slipper from the footman. "Look!" she cried "A perfect fit."

"No it is not!" shouted the other stepsister. "Your heel is hanging out. Give it to me!" She snatched the glass slipper.

It didn't fit her either, though she tried to pretend that it did.

"Is there anyone else in the house who should try the slipper?" asked the footman.

"No!" said both stepsisters together.

"Yes there is," said their father. "Cinderella has not tried it yet."

"The Prince would never marry HER!" laughed the stepsisters.

"The Prince said everyone must try the slipper," said the footman.

It fitted Cinderella perfectly. Her stepsisters were so suprised they fainted.

The stepsisters still looked surprised when the Prince and Cinderella were married.

Pinocchio

Old Geppetto was making a puppet. As he cut the wood he heard a voice.

"Please do not hurt me," it said.

Geppetto looked all around. He could not see anyone so he went on with his work. When he made the puppet's eyes, they moved. When he made the mouth, it laughed. When he made the feet, they kicked.

"You are just like a real boy," said Geppetto.

He called the puppet Pinocchio.

Geppetto showed Pinocchio how to walk. Naughty Pinocchio ran into the street. Geppetto ran after him. A policeman thought Geppetto was being unkind. He took Geppetto to the police station.

Pinocchio went home. He was very pleased with himself.

"Boys who run away are sorry in the end," said a talking cricket. Pinocchio threw a hammer at the cricket.

"I am taking no notice of you," he said.

Pinocchio went out in the rain to find some food. Nobody would give him any. He went home hungry. He sat by the fire and fell asleep.

Geppetto knocked at the door. Pinocchio got up to answer it. He fell to the floor. "The fire has eaten my feet," he cried.

Geppetto climbed in through the window. "Don't worry, Pinocchio," said Geppetto. "I will make you some new feet. First we shall have something to eat."

Pinocchio was very pleased with his new feet. "I shall go to school and make you proud of me," he said to Geppetto. "But I need a reading book."

Geppetto sold his coat to buy the reading book.

On his way to school Pinocchio saw a puppet theatre. He sold his book and paid to go in. He forgot all about school. He stayed all day and all night.

The puppet man gave him five gold coins to take home.

On the way home Pinocchio met a fox and a cat. The fox pretended to be lame. The cat pretended to be blind. They tried to trick Pinocchio out of his gold coins. Pinocchio ran away from them.

The fox and the cat chased him. They caught him and tied him to a tree. He was rescued by a fairy. She took him home. "How did this happen?" she asked.

Pinocchio started to tell her the truth but he said he had lost the five gold coins. They were not lost. They were in his pocket. His nose began to grow. His nose grew because he was telling lies.

His nose grew very long indeed. He could not get it through the door.

At last the fairy took pity on him. She called some woodpeckers. The woodpeckers pecked his nose back to the right size.

Pinocchio wanted to see Geppetto. "I shall go home now," said Pinocchio. On the way he met the fox and the cat. This time they stole his money. Pinocchio told a

policeman. The policeman did not believe him. He put Pinocchio in prison.

A long time later Pinocchio came out of prison. He went looking for Geppetto again. Geppetto was looking for Pinocchio. He went to sea in a boat.

Pinocchio went to the seashore. He saw Geppetto's boat tossed on the waves. He swam out to help him.

Pinocchio met a dolphin in the sea. "Geppetto has been swallowed by a sea monster," said the dolphin.

Pinocchio sadly swam on. He reached an island and met the fairy. "I don't want to be a puppet," said Pinocchio. "I want to be a boy."

"You can be a boy if you are good," said the fairy. "First you must go to school."

Pinocchio tried to be good but it was too hard. He ran away to Toyland with some other naughty boys. In Toyland they were all so lazy they soon turned into donkeys. Pinocchio was sold to a circus. In the circus ring Pinocchio fell and hurt his leg.

He was thrown into the sea to drown. But he turned back into a puppet. A sea monster swallowed him.

What a surprise! There inside the fish Pinocchio found Geppetto. They hugged each other.

"We can escape when the monster is asleep," said Pinocchio. They swam out of the monster's mouth. From that day on Pinocchio looked after Geppetto.

Finally the fairy granted his wish. She made him into a real boy.

The Little Mermaid

The King of the Sea and his family live in a palace on the seabed. Fish swim in and out of the palace all the time. The King's family have tails like the fish.

The King's daughters are the mermaids. They find things from shipwrecks. They put them in their gardens. One little mermaid has a statue of a boy in her garden.

Her grandmother tells her stories. The little mermaid likes stories about people.

When mermaids grow up they can go to the surface of the sea. This is the first time the little mermaid has been to the surface. The sea is shiny and flat, like glass. She can see a ship.

There is a prince on the ship. He is like the statue of the boy in her garden.

The wind begins to blow. There is a storm coming. It starts to rain. The ship is tossed by the waves. Suddenly the ship turns over. It is sinking. The prince is thrown into the water. He is drowning.

The little mermaid does not want the prince to drown. She puts her arms round him. She stops him sinking. The waves take them to the shore. The little mermaid lays the prince on the sand. His eyes are closed but he is alive.

There is someone coming. The little mermaid hides behind a rock. She sees some girls. The girls see the

prince. They do not see the little mermaid. They carry the prince away.

The little mermaid goes home to the palace under the sea. She sits in her garden and looks at the statue of the boy. She thinks about the prince all the time.

Her mermaid sisters find out where the prince is living. They take the little mermaid to the place.

The little mermaid visits the bay every night. She watches the prince. She cannot go to him because she cannot walk. She has no feet. Every night she is more sad. "I will ask the witch to change my tail into legs and feet," she says. "Then perhaps the prince will love me."

"I will help if you give me your voice," says the witch. The little mermaid loves to sing but she loves the prince more. "You will die if the prince ever loves another better than you!" warns the witch.

"Please do as I ask," says the little mermaid. The witch mixes her a potion.

The little mermaid swims to the bay where the prince lives. She drags herself on to the sand. She drinks the potion and faints.

When the little mermaid opens her eyes, the prince is standing beside her. "Who are you?" he asks. "Where have you come from?"

She cannot answer because she has no voice.

The prince takes her to his palace. Her new feet hurt with every step she takes.

The little mermaid dances gracefully. Nobody knows how much her new feet hurt.

When the prince goes riding, he takes the little mermaid with him. At night she sleeps on a velvet cushion outside his door.

One night, when everyone is asleep, she goes to bathe her feet in the sea. Her sisters come to see her. They tell her they miss her. Her father and her grandmother are missing her too. They wave to her from some way off.

The prince grows to love the little mermaid like a sister. She is very happy. Then, one day, the King sends the prince to see a princess. The prince does not want to go. The King says he must.

As soon as the prince sees the princess he wants to marry her. The little mermaid remembers what the witch said. She is very sad. She knows she will die. On the day of the wedding everyone is happy, except for the little mermaid.

After the wedding they go on board a ship. The little mermaid's sisters follow the ship. They have cut off their long hair. "We have found a way to save you," they call to the little mermaid. "We have given the witch our hair. In return she has given us a knife which will break the spell."

Then the sisters shout to the little mermaid, "You must kill the prince. His blood must fall on your feet. Then your feet will turn back into a tail. You will be a mermaid again and you can come back to our palace under the sea."

The little mermaid looks at the sleeping prince. She cannot harm him. She would rather die herself. The little mermaid throws the knife into the sea. Then she throws herself into the sea. She changes into sparkling foam and is never seen again.

Aladdin

Once there was a magician. He went to China to look for a magic lamp. The lamp was in a cave. The way into the cave was along a tunnel. To touch the walls of the tunnel meant certain death. The magician wanted the lamp but he was afraid to go along the tunnel.

"I will ask someone else to get the lamp for me," said the magician. He asked a boy called Aladdin. The magician did not tell Aladdin he would die if he touched the walls of the tunnel.

Aladdin said he would get the lamp. Aladdin was ready to go. The magician gave him a ring.

"Wear this," said the magician. "It will keep you safe."

"Safe from what?" asked Aladdin.

"Er … nothing," said the magician. "You will find the lamp at the back of the cave."

Aladdin was away for a long time.

"He must have touched the walls of the tunnel. He must be dead," said the magician. Then he saw Aladdin coming back. "Give me the the lamp," said the magician.

Aladdin put the lamp up his sleeve. "Help me out of the tunnel first," he said.

"Give me the lamp," said the magician. "Then I will help you out of the tunnel."

Aladdin did not trust the magician. "No!" he said. "Help me out first."

The magician became angry. "If you will not give me the lamp you can stay there forever!" he said. Then he closed the mouth of the tunnel with a magic spell.

Aladdin was trapped. He did not know what to do. By chance he rubbed the ring on his finger. There was a puff of smoke. A genie appeared.

"Who are you? What do you want?" asked Aladdin.

"I am the Genie of the Ring. Your wish is my command," said the genie.

"Then take me home," said Aladdin.

Suddenly Aladdin was at home. He did not know how he had got there. The lamp was still up his sleeve. "We can sell this and buy food," he said.

"I will clean it first," said his mother. Aladdin's mother rubbed at the lamp. There was a puff of smoke. A genie appeared. Aladdin's mother was afraid. She hid her face.

Aladdin was not afraid. "Who are you?" he asked.

"I am the Genie of the Lamp," said the genie. "Your wish is my command." The genie gave Aladdin everything he asked for.

Time went by. Aladdin had fine clothes to wear. He lived in a palace. He had a princess for a wife.

One day Aladdin went hunting. The princess was in the palace alone. She heard a pedlar calling. "New lamps for old!" he cried.

"I will change Aladdin's old lamp for a new one," said the princess. Aladdin had not told her it was a magic lamp.

"She took the lamp and gave it to the pedlar. The pedlar had the lamp in his hand. He threw off his ragged coat. The pedlar was really the magician.

"Now everything Aladdin has shall be mine," he said. He rubbed the magic lamp.

"What is your command, master?" asked the Genie of the Lamp.

"Take the princess, myself, the palace and everything in it to Africa," said the magician. The genie had to obey the command.

Aladdin came home. There was nothing where the palace had been. Aladdin guessed what had happened. He rubbed the magic ring.

"What is your command, master?" asked the Genie of the Ring.

"Bring back my princess and my palace!" said Aladdin.

"Only the Genie of the Lamp can do that, master."

"Then take me to my princess," said Aladdin.

The princess was glad to see Aladdin. "Where is the magic lamp?"asked Aladdin.

"The magician has it up his sleeve," said the princess.

"Put this powder in his wine," said Aladdin. "It will make him sleep." The princess did as Aladdin asked.

When the magician was asleep, Aladdin took the lamp. The princess was afraid the magician would wake up. "Please be careful," she said.

Aladdin rubbed the lamp with his sleeve. The genie appeared. "What is your command, master?" asked the genie.

"Take the palace and everyone in it back to China. But leave the magician here in Africa," said Aladdin.

The magician woke up. "Where is the palace?" he said. "Where is the princess?"

He looked up his sleeve for the magic lamp. It was gone. He would have to walk back to China.

The magician never did get back to China. Aladdin and his princess lived happily ever after.

The Snow Queen

Once there was a boy called Kay and girl called Gerda. They were friends. They played together.

One winter's day, Kay's grandmother told them about the Snow Queen. "The Snow Queen brings the snow and ice," she said.

Kay thought he could see the Snow Queen's face at the window. She seemed to be calling to him. He was afraid. He did not go.

The next day Kay went out with his sledge. He saw a bigger sledge. He tied his sledge to it for a ride.

The big sledge set off. It went faster and faster and far away. When the sledge stopped, Kay saw who was driving it. It was the Snow Queen.

The Snow Queen kissed Kay. "My kiss will put ice in your heart," she said. "You will forget your home. You will forget Gerda." She took Kay to her palace.

Gerda wept when she could not find Kay. She went to the river. "I will give you my new red shoes," she said to the river. "Please tell me where Kay is."

The river said nothing.

Gerda stepped into a boat. The boat began to move. The river was moving the boat.

An old woman pulled in the boat. She cast a spell on Gerda to make her forget Kay.

But one day Gerda saw a painted rose. It made her think of him. "I must find Kay," she said and off she ran.

Gerda met a raven. She told the raven her story. The raven knew of a prince. "Perhaps he is Kay," said the raven.

The raven took Gerda to the palace to see the prince. But the prince was not Kay.

Gerda left the castle in a coach.

Robbers attacked the coach. Gerda's life was saved by a little robber girl. Gerda told the robber girl she was looking for Kay.

The robber girl said, "I will help you if I can."

That night a bird said to Gerda, "I have seen Kay. He was with the Snow Queen."

"Where were they going?" asked Gerda.

"To the Land of Snow and Ice," said the bird.

"I come from that land," said a reindeer. It belonged to the robber girl. "I can take you there," it said.

The robber girl agreed to set the reindeer free. "Take Gerda to find Kay," she said.

After many days they came to the Land of Snow and Ice. They went to see a wise old woman. She told the reindeer, "You must leave Gerda at the Snow Queen's garden."

The reindeer did this.

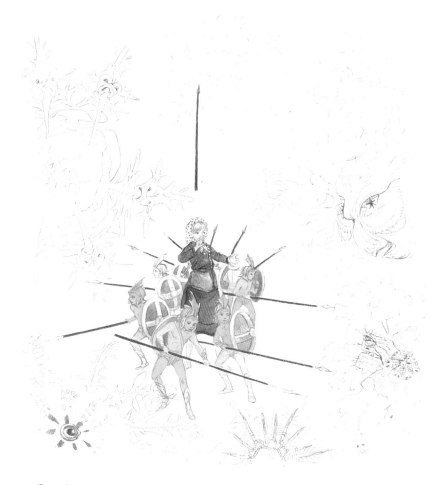

Gerda was alone. The Snow Queen's guards tried to frighten her away. Little angels came to keep her safe.

Gerda went into the palace. The Snow Queen was away. Kay was all alone. Gerda ran to greet him. "Kay," she cried. "Do you not know me? I am Gerda."

Kay did not move or speak. He did not know her.

Gerda cried. Her hot tears fell all over Kay. They melted the ice in his heart. Now he knew who Gerda was. Then Kay cried too.

"We must run away from here," said Kay. They ran to the garden. The reindeer was waiting.

The reindeer carried them away. They were safe from the Snow Queen and they lived happily ever after.